CONTENTS

Welcome aboard the
SPECTACULAR

*You're sure to have an amazing cruise
holiday on board the Spectacular.
The name of the ship says it all!*

It truly is a spectacular cruise liner, with a huge range of activities to suit both kids and adults. There are restaurants and cafés catering to all tastes, and of course, luxurious cabins for a good night's sleep. All this, plus the sea and sun of the tropics!

We'll be sailing around the Bahamas – an archipelago of about 700 heavenly islands dotted across more than 100,000 square miles of the Caribbean Sea. Only 30 of these islands are developed. You can explore the lush tropical paradise and perfect white beaches of these islands at each port of call when we dock.

So relax and enjoy your Spectacular cruise!

Relax in the tropical sun on the ship's deck.

Swim in five
refreshing pools.

Enjoy the luxury and
splendour of the ship!

Exercise in our
state-of-the-art gym.

For Kids

Activities and entertainment

Choose from a variety
of sports for all ages.

Zoom down the
water slides!

Have fun playing
games on deck.

Be dazzled by our on-board entertainment!

Chapter 1

Sea, Sun and Fun

"I can't believe how enormous this cruise ship is," said Marina.

"It's like a whole city on a great big boat," agreed her younger brother, Jason.

It was their second day on a luxury cruise with their dad. They were standing on the top deck of the *Spectacular* as the huge liner sailed out of the port on Grand Bahama Island.

The *Spectacular* was an appropriate name for the cruise ship. It had a total of 15 decks with rooms for more than 3,000 passengers, plus lots of restaurants and all

sorts of activities and entertainment.
On the top deck there were swimming
pools, an amazing playground and even
a water park.

"The *Spectacular* sure is spectacular,"
said Dad.

"Haha." Marina couldn't help grinning.
"You've made that joke about a hundred
times since we left Miami."

"Grand Bahama Island was pretty
spectacular, too, wasn't it?" said Dad.

"Oh no, I forgot to send Mum's
postcard!" Marina pulled it out of her bag.

Dear Mum,
The cruise is a lot of fun
and Dad's taking good care
of us, so don't worry. This
postcard is from our first
port of call, Grand Bahama
Island. It's a tropical
paradise! See you next
week.
Lots of love,
Marina and Jason

"You can send it from the next port," said Dad. "We're scheduled to dock at Great Abaco Island tomorrow afternoon."

"Dad, how does the ship stay afloat?" Jason piped up. "It's so big you'd think it would sink."

"Why don't you ask the Captain at dinner tonight?" said Dad. "We've had a special invitation to sit at the Captain's table this evening."

"Okay," said Jason. He was quiet for a moment. "What if the ship does sink?"

"We had the safety drill yesterday, remember?" Dad pointed out.

"You mean the muster drill," Jason corrected.

"That's right. They told us that if there's an emergency, we're to go straight to the muster stations. Ours is 5A. Look, it's even on your wristbands so you can't forget."

Dad pointed to the special cruise wristbands that Jason and Marina were wearing. "Besides, there are plenty of life jackets and lifeboats on board. Don't worry, Jason."

"Anyway, I'm sure modern ships like this are unsinkable," said Marina confidently.

"That's what people said about the *Titanic*," Jason replied, "and everyone knows about the sinking of that ship."

"Didn't it hit an iceberg?" asked Dad.

"That's right," said Jason, "and then it sank to the bottom of the ocean."

"There aren't likely to be any icebergs here in the tropics, so don't worry," said Dad. "Just feel that hot sun."

"Yeah, enjoy the cruise, Jason," Marina agreed. "Come on, let's all cool off at the water park!"

Quickly they went to their cabin to change into swimming gear and hurried back to the top deck where the water park shimmered in the sunlight. Marina and Jason climbed up the tall steps to wait their turn on the giant water slide. Dad waved to them from the pool.

"Look, Jason," said Marina, pointing to the sea below. "Are they dolphins?"

"It's a pod of dolphins!" exclaimed Jason. "They're swimming alongside the ship."

They watched the dolphins until it was their turn to go down the slide. Marina went first. The ocean looked like a big blue blur as she zoomed around. The slide dipped and turned like a roller coaster until at last Marina neared the end. It seemed as if she might zoom right into the ocean, but then the slide veered again, and she jumped into the cool water of the swimming pool. Jason followed, splashing into the pool with a shriek.

The children and Dad spent all afternoon at the water park. At last they headed back towards their cabin on Deck 7. Instead of taking the lift, they decided to go down the stairs on the outer decks of the ship so they could see the dolphins.

They went down several flights of stairs, keeping an eye on the sea next to the ship as they went, but there was no sign of the dolphins. Then suddenly, a big group of dolphins appeared together, resuming their swim alongside the ship.

"Look how many dolphins there are!" Marina exclaimed, looking over the railing. "There must be at least 50 of them down there."

"They look like bottlenose dolphins," said Jason, as he and Dad joined her at the railing to watch them. "You can tell from their short, thick beaks."

"When did you become a dolphin expert?" asked Marina.

Jason shrugged. "I read a book about dolphins. It had lots of cool facts in it."

Suddenly, one of the dolphins leaped out of the water. As it dived back under the water, it slapped its tail on the surface. Another dolphin leaped out of the water, and then another.

Marina watched in wonder. The dolphins were so beautiful and graceful, and they almost seemed to be smiling.

"I think they're putting on a show for us," said Dad.

"Maybe they're saying something," said Jason. "My book said that dolphins might use body language to communicate."

The dolphins finished leaping and diving, and swam away in their pod towards the horizon.

"Look at that!" Marina pointed. "They're swimming in formation, like synchronised swimmers."

Marina, Jason and Dad clapped.

"Bravo! Bravo!" Dad called to the dolphins. "Encore!"

Marina laughed as she watched the dolphins disappear into the distance. Then she settled herself into a deck chair. She loved the rhythm of the gently bobbing waves that lapped at the sides of the ship, and the way the sea glistened in the late afternoon sun. In the distance, some puffy clouds cast their shadows over the water.

Jason sat next to her. "I wonder what the dolphins were trying to tell us."

Bottlenose Dolphins

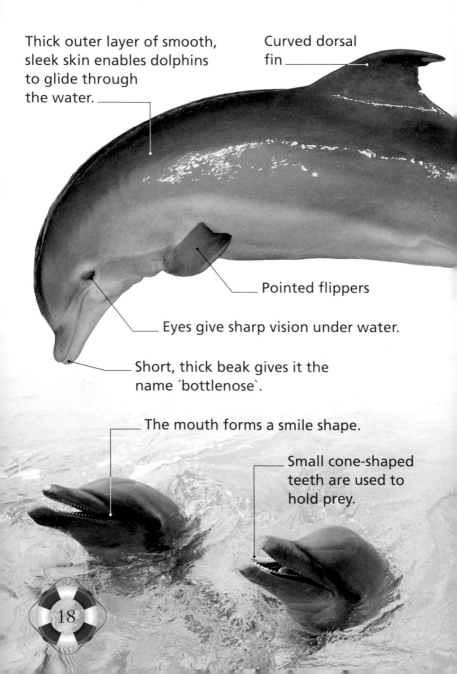

Thick outer layer of smooth, sleek skin enables dolphins to glide through the water.

Curved dorsal fin

Pointed flippers

Eyes give sharp vision under water.

Short, thick beak gives it the name 'bottlenose'.

The mouth forms a smile shape.

Small cone-shaped teeth are used to hold prey.

IIII Dolphin Facts IIIIIIIIIIIIIIIIIIIIIIIIIIIIIIIIIIIIIIIII

Length
1.9–4 m (6–13 feet)

Weight
can be up to
500 kg (1,100 lbs)

Colour
light blue to slate grey
with pale underside

The tail is
called a fluke.

■ Dolphins are mammals. They breathe air, but can stay under water for 4–5 minutes.

■ A female dolphin is a 'cow'. A male is a 'bull' and a baby is a 'calf'.

■ A group of dolphins is a 'pod' or 'school'. There can be 10–100 dolphins in a pod.

■ Bottlenose dolphins live in oceans and seas around the world, except for polar regions. They eat a varied diet of fish, squid and shellfish.

■ They can leap high into the air in a move called a 'breach' and slap the water with their tails. This may be a form of communication or simply playful behaviour.

■ These curious, intelligent animals are known to interact with humans.

■ Dolphins often swim alongside ships, using the waves created by the ship to conserve energy.

19

How does a Heavy Ship Float?

Climb into a bath of water and you'll notice the water level rise. The water is pushed aside, or displaced, to make space for you. More than 2,000 years ago, a Greek scientist called Archimedes found that the weight of water displaced by an object equals the weight of the object itself. However, an object weighs less in water because the upward force of the water, or buoyancy, partly supports the object.

This means that the downward force of a ship's weight has to balance with the upward force of the displaced water. The secret is that the hull of a ship takes up a lot of space, but its weight is less than the weight of the water it displaces, enabling the ship to float.

Try this experiment to see how the ship floats

You will need: glass marble; modelling clay; container of water

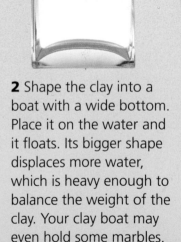

1 Drop the marble into the water. It sinks because the weight of the marble causes a downward force that is greater than the upward force of the water being displaced. Drop a ball of modelling clay into the water and it sinks too.

2 Shape the clay into a boat with a wide bottom. Place it on the water and it floats. Its bigger shape displaces more water, which is heavy enough to balance the weight of the clay. Your clay boat may even hold some marbles.

THE SINKING OF THE **TITANIC**

On 10th April, 1912, the *Titanic* set sail on its maiden (first) voyage from Southampton, England, bound for New York City. It was a large, luxurious ship and people said it was ´unsinkable`. The journey was expected to take one week.

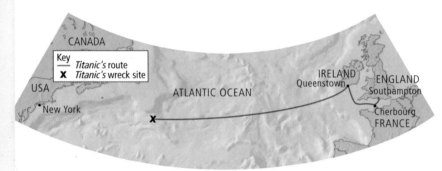

The night of 14th April was clear and cold. The sea was calm. The *Titanic* was sailing at full-speed. At about 11:40 p.m., lookout Frederick Fleet, who was keeping watch from high up in the crow's nest, spotted an iceberg ahead and rang the warning bell. First Officer William Murdoch was in charge of the ship at the time. He told Quartermaster Robert Hichens to turn the ship's wheel, but the huge liner couldn't avoid the iceberg. The *Titanic* struck the iceberg on the starboard (right) side of the hull.

The collision only caused minor damage to the upper decks, but below the surface of the sea, the iceberg punched a series of gashes and holes along the hull, which started filling up with water. Just after midnight, Captain Edward Smith gave the order to abandon ship.

Within three hours, the *Titanic* sank. Sadly, more than 1,500 people died, due to a lack of safety procedures and a shortage of lifeboats on the ´unsinkable` *Titanic*. (See pages 70–71 for more information.)

23

Chapter 2

The Ship's Captain

That evening Marina and Jason put on their best clothes for dinner at the Captain's table. When they saw what their dad was wearing, they erupted with laughter.

"Don't I look nice?" he asked, straightening his bowtie.

"You look like a penguin, Dad!" Jason spluttered.

"We've never seen you in a dinner jacket before," Marina giggled.

Dad grinned. "Well, I understand that dinner at the Captain's table is very posh.

It's an honour to be invited, so we've all got to be on our best behaviour."

They took the lift to Deck 14, where they were ushered into a restaurant called *Belle Mer*.

"It means 'beautiful sea'," Marina translated for Jason.

A waiter showed them to the Captain's table, laid with a white tablecloth, china dishes and crystal glasses. Candles flickered in the centre. The other guests wore elegant dresses or dinner jackets like Dad's.

"I told you it was posh," he whispered.

They found place cards with their names and took their seats. Dad chatted away to the elderly woman next to him, who introduced herself as Pearl. Marina sat on Dad's other side, and then Jason. He glanced at the empty chair next to him and was delighted to find that the place card said 'Captain MacGill'.

Jason fidgeted with his tie as he waited for the captain to arrive. At last she strode into the dining room, wearing navy-coloured trousers and a white jacket with four stripes on each shoulder.

"Good evening, all," she said. "I'm sorry I'm late."

Captain MacGill shook hands with everyone at the table, including Marina and Jason, and then sat down.

"Excuse me, Captain," said Jason.

She smiled at him. "Yes, young man?"

"Is there a problem with the ship?" asked Jason. "Is that why you were late?"

"We just needed to make some adjustments to our route. Nothing out of the ordinary," Captain MacGill answered.

"What is our route exactly?" asked Jason. "I know we're sailing around the Bahama Islands, but I'd like to see a map."

"Don't mind my brother," Marina piped up. "He likes to know everything."

?

Why does Jason want to see a map?

"So do I." Captain MacGill winked at Jason and reached into the pocket of her jacket. "As a matter of fact, I've got a map right here."

She unfolded it and smoothed it out on the table so Jason and Marina could see.

"We sailed from Miami yesterday," said Captain MacGill, pointing to the city of Miami on the coast of Florida. "Today we docked in Freeport on Grand Bahama, which is here."

Jason nodded as he looked at the map.

"Then we'll sail to the islands of Great

Abaco, Eleuthera and Andros," Captain MacGill continued, "before finally heading back to Miami."

Jason studied the map. "Where's Bermuda?" he asked.

The Captain pointed to an island that was in the Atlantic Ocean, northeast of the Caribbean. "It's here, but this cruise doesn't sail to Bermuda."

"I know," said Jason, nodding. "And this is Puerto Rico?" he asked, pointing to an island in the Caribbean Sea.

"That's right," said the Captain, "but we won't be going there either."

"This is the Bermuda Triangle, isn't it?" said Jason. "I read about it in a book. It's dangerous. And we're sailing inside it."

Marina looked over his shoulder as Jason leaned over the map and used his fingers to make a triangle with Bermuda, Puerto Rico and Miami at the points.

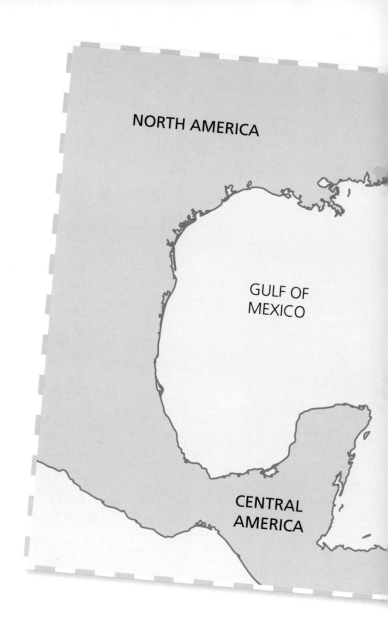

NORTH AMERICA

GULF OF
MEXICO

CENTRAL
AMERICA

30

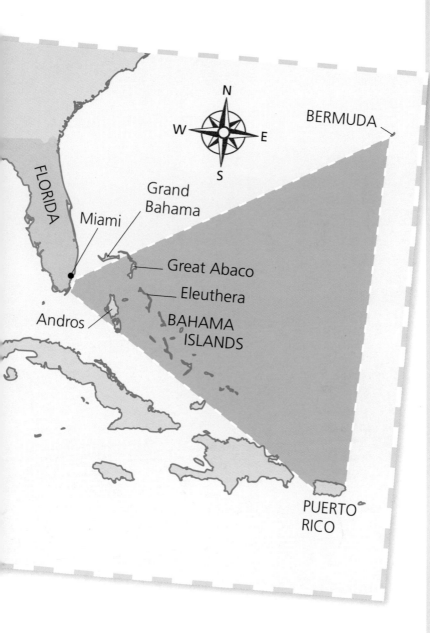

N

W   E

S

BERMUDA

FLORIDA

Miami

Grand
Bahama

Great Abaco

Eleuthera

Andros

BAHAMA
ISLANDS

PUERTO
RICO

Marina looked at the area marked as the Bahama Islands, which was just inside the western edge of Jason's triangle.

"So what, Jason?" she said impatiently. "Nothing's going to happen to us."

"There's no proof that there are more shipwrecks here than in any other part of the ocean," said Captain MacGill.

"See?" Marina looked at her brother. "I told you, the ship is unsinkable."

"Technically, no ship is unsinkable," said the Captain, "but the *Spectacular* is certainly seaworthy, with the most up-to-date equipment."

Just then, dinner was served and the Captain folded up her map. "Would you like to come and see the bridge after dinner? It's the control centre of the ship."

"Yes, please!" said Jason and Marina together.

After five courses, dinner at the Captain's table was finally over.

Captain MacGill led the children to the bridge, which was a room on the top deck of the ship. It had huge windows all around, where Jason and Marina could see the ocean stretching out in every direction beneath the darkening sky. Computer screens, buttons and levers filled the ship's control panel. It reminded Marina of the cockpit of an aeroplane.

Captain MacGill introduced them to officers who worked on the bridge. "Most of the time, the ship's controls are on autopilot," she explained, "but we need to keep a close watch. We work in shifts so there are always bridge officers on duty."

"Captain," called the Chief Radio Officer, "look at this satellite picture." Jason and Marina peered behind the captain so they could see too. "There's a tropical storm heading north from the equator towards the Caribbean."

"It's miles away, but let's keep an eye on it," said the Captain. "The storm shouldn't cause us a problem unless it turns into a full-blown hurricane. That would be very unlikely this early in the season."

Marina looked out through the huge windows of the bridge. She could see dark clouds scudding across the moon in the night sky. The enormous sea looked almost black except for the white foam of the large waves that rose and fell around the ship. They were quite different from the gently bobbing waves she saw earlier.

THE MYSTERY OF THE
BERMUDA TRIANGLE

The Bermuda Triangle is about 500,000 square miles (1,295 sq km) in area. It is not marked on official maps and the United States Coast Guard 'does not recognise the existence of the so-called Bermuda Triangle as a geographic area of specific hazard to ships or planes'. However, many mysterious happenings have been reported there. These are just a few.

GHOST SHIP

Sailing through the Bermuda Triangle to Canada in 1881, the crew of the *Ellen Austin* spotted a ship in trouble. They were surprised to find no one on board. With some of the *Ellen Austin* crew sailing the ghost ship, they set sail together, but the ghost ship mysteriously disappeared in a bank of thick fog. When the *Ellen Austin* finally found the ghost ship, the crew had vanished.

36

Disappearing aircraft

Several months after the end of World War II in 1945, five Avenger torpedo bombers took off from Fort Lauderdale, Florida over the Bermuda Triangle on a routine flying mission. The Flight Leader radioed for help, but the five aircraft and 14 crew members were never seen again. During the search mission, one of the searching aircraft also disappeared.

EERIE YELLOW HAZE

A group of experienced pilots flew a small aircraft through the Bermuda Triangle in 1986. Suddenly the clear blue sky became an eerie yellow haze and the aircraft instruments stopped working. Through the thick haze, a narrow tunnel led to the sea below. After several hours, the eerie yellow haze suddenly vanished and they were surrounded once more by clear blue sky.

Gone fishing

In 2008, Phillip Fredericks set sail from St. John in the Virgin Islands, heading for Puerto Rico in his fishing boat. Despite having a powerful outboard engine, flares, life jackets and two mobile phones, Fredericks and his boat disappeared. Even after an intensive air and sea search by the United States Coast Guard, neither Fredericks nor the boat has ever been found.

BERMUDA TRIANGLE THEORIES

Are these incidents in the Bermuda Triangle the result of supernatural activity or is there another explanation?

Supernatural theories

The lost island of Atlantis

In ancient Greek mythology, Atlantis was a great island civilisation that sank beneath the sea. Some people believe it is near the island of Bimini in the Bermuda Triangle, and that traces of energy crystals from Atlantis can interfere with instruments on ships and aircraft.

Aliens and UFOs

Are aliens from other worlds kidnapping human beings from the Bermuda Triangle? This would explain the weird lights sometimes seen in the skies over the Triangle, and the disappearance of people without a trace.

Portal to another dimension

Is the Bermuda Triangle a portal linking this world with another dimension? Perhaps those who are missing have travelled to another time or place not usually accessible by earthlings.

Other theories

Gulf Stream
The Gulf Stream is a powerful ocean current passing through the Bermuda Triangle. It can make navigation difficult and sweep away the wreckage of ships, making them almost impossible to find.

Ocean floor maze
The ocean floor is a maze of shallow water and deep-sea trenches plus many islands, including those that are submerged below the waterline and difficult to detect.

Magnetic mix-ups
The Bermuda Triangle is one of only two areas in the world where a magnetic compass points true north instead of magnetic north, making navigation more difficult.

Pirates
The area has long been frequented by pirates. Who knows – maybe they're involved in the eerie happenings in the Bermuda Triangle?

Wild weather
The Bermuda Triangle is known for rapid changes in weather. Hurricanes are common between June and November, while water spouts are quick but deadly tornadoes at sea that whip up water from the ocean's surface.

Methane gas
Pockets of concentrated methane gas are trapped under the ocean floor. When they erupt, the water becomes much less dense. This creates a vacuum that could pull a boat under the surface. Sediment might then cover the boat to hide it.

WHAT
DO YOU
THINK?

CRUISE SHIP
CLASSIFIED ADVERTISEMENTS

WOULD YOU LIKE TO WORK ON A CRUISE SHIP?

You must:
- ✔ like travelling and meeting new people,
- ✔ be able to handle long working hours,
- ✔ NOT be prone to seasickness.

All except top jobs require staff to share small cabins.

The deck

Experienced sailors responsible for safe navigation of the ship and the safety of everyone on board.

CAPTAIN In charge of the entire ship and the safety of all passengers.

STAFF CAPTAIN Second-in-command to the captain.

FIRST OFFICER Supervises the bridge.

CHIEF RADIO OFFICER Responsible for the ship's communications regarding weather, traffic and safety.

NAVIGATION OFFICER Navigates a safe route for the ship.

QUARTERMASTER Keeps watch on the bridge and steers the ship as directed by the officer in charge of the bridge.

BOATSWAIN (also known as a bosun) Supervises ship maintenance and has a key role in mooring and anchoring.

ABLE SEAMAN Performs routine ship maintenance and operates lifeboats and other safety equipment.

Other cruise ship jobs

ENGINE STAFF Mechanics, engineers, plumbers, electricians, etc., keep the ship running in good order.

ENTERTAINMENT STAFF Organise a wide range of on-board entertainment.

ACTIVITIES AND YOUTH STAFF Plan passenger activities including parties, games, etc., for children.

MEDICAL STAFF Look after the health of everyone on the ship.

CLEANING AND HOUSEKEEPING STAFF Take care of passengers and their cabins.

SPA AND SALON STAFF Fitness instructors, hairdressers, manicurists, etc.

CATERING STAFF Chefs, servers and dish-washers for on-board cafés and restaurants.

RETAIL STAFF Managers and assistants for a wide variety of on-board shops.

Chapter 3

Choppy Seas

The next morning Marina and Jason were woken up by the rolling of the ship from side to side and up and down. The floor of their cabin slanted first one way and then another so that it was hard to stand upright.

"It's like an amusement park ride," laughed Marina, as she lost her balance and flopped onto the bed.

Jason held tightly to the railing with one hand and tried to pull his clothes on with the other.

"It's not funny," he said. "Those waves

must be really choppy out there."

Dad staggered out of the bathroom, clutching a sick bag.

"Are you okay, Dad?" asked Marina.

"You look a bit green," Jason observed.

"I feel seasick." Dad lay down on his bed. "I'd better stay here until the sea calms down and my head stops spinning. You two go upstairs and get breakfast."

"Are you sure?" asked Marina.

Dad nodded weakly.

"Hope you feel better soon, Dad," said Jason as he followed his sister out of the cabin.

Marina and Jason decided to go to the brunch buffet on Deck 11. They wanted to take the stairs on the outer decks so they could check if the dolphins were there, but the outer decks were closed. Through the glass door that separated the inside and outside areas of the ship, they could see big waves crashing over the railing, sloshing water across the deck.

As they watched the waves, an

announcement came over the ship's public address system.

"Good morning, passengers and crew. This is Captain MacGill speaking. I'm sure you've noticed that the wind has picked up and the ship is sailing through very choppy seas at the moment. This is due to a tropical storm nearby. We were aiming to outrun the storm during the night, but I'm afraid it's catching up with us so we're changing our route slightly to find a port where we can sit out the storm. Please note that the outer decks and pool decks are closed for safety reasons, but otherwise continue as normal. Thank you."

Marina sighed. "I hope the dolphins will be okay in the tropical storm."

"I think they'll be fine. After all, dolphins are used to living in the ocean," Jason replied. "It's us I'm worried about. I'll feel better once we've docked at another port and we're back on dry land."

On the lift up to Deck 11, everyone clung to the railings as it rocked and pitched along with the movement of the ship. Marina thought again of a wild amusement park ride.

At the brunch buffet, customers could choose what they wanted from the long tables covered with food. Marina and Jason each picked up a tray from the stack and looked at the menu.

SPECTACULAR
Brunch Buffet

Selection of juices

Coffee, tea, hot cocoa

Caribbean fruit salad

Toast, croissants, bagels and pastries

Eggs and omelettes made to order

Pancakes with a choice of toppings

Bacon, sausages and hash browns

Marina chose pancakes, while Jason thought the tropical fruit in the Caribbean fruit salad looked interesting. As he went to spoon it into his bowl, the ship rolled and the fruit ended up on the tray instead. All around them, people clutched their trays of food to prevent the dishes from falling off.

Suddenly they felt the ship go up and over another big wave, and the stack of trays fell over with a loud crash! As Marina turned to look, the pancakes slid off her tray and into the lap of an elderly woman sitting at a nearby table!

"I'm so sorry," Marina apologised.

The woman smiled. "It's okay, dear. Things get a little crazy in choppy seas like this." She cleaned the pancakes off her skirt and dabbed at the orange juice.

"I'm Pearl, by the way. I met you and your father at the Captain's table last night. Why don't you two sit down before the rest of your breakfast goes flying?"

She gestured to the other seats at the table. Jason sat and started eating, while Marina went to get more pancakes. This time, she was extra careful.

"I love the sea, although I prefer it when it's calm." Pearl laughed as the ship rolled again and her croissant nearly slid off the table. "Jason and Marina are very special names, you know. Marina means 'lady of the sea'."

Marina grinned. "The lady of the sea – that sounds mysterious, doesn't it?"

"What about my name?" asked Jason.

"Jason was the hero of a Greek myth," Pearl told him. "He sailed to far-off places and performed amazing feats."

Jason's eyes opened wide. "Wow, I'm a hero. Cool!"

Marina laughed. "Don't get carried away, Jason. You haven't performed any amazing feats."

"Some day I will," Jason insisted.

Just then, they heard the Captain's voice over the public address system.

"This is an urgent announcement. Would all passengers please return to their cabins as soon as possible. The tropical storm that I mentioned earlier has grown stronger. We're measuring the wind speed at 75 mph, which means the storm is now classified as a hurricane. Unfortunately, it also means that the wind is too strong for the ship to dock. So we're going to head out to sea and wait for the hurricane to pass. Please stay calm and return to your cabins. Thank you."

Marina and Jason looked at each other in alarm. She grabbed his hand. Jason reached out for Pearl's hand too, and together they joined the crowd that was hurrying out of the dining room.

"Don't worry, Jason," Marina told her brother. "I'm sure the hurricane will pass soon." But inside, she wasn't so sure.

Jason and the Argonauts

LONG AGO IN ANCIENT GREECE, a young man called Jason arrived in the kingdom of Iolkos. He was determined to win back the throne that his uncle, King Pelias, had seized from his father many years before.

"Of course you may be king," Pelias told Jason, "if you retrieve the fleece of the golden ram from King Aietes, ruler of the distant kingdom of Colchis." Pelias gave an evil grin, for he knew that the golden fleece was guarded by a deadly serpent.

Jason had a fabulous ship built for the voyage and gathered many brave warriors to help him. The ship was called the *Argo*, and the warriors were the Argonauts. At last Jason set off on his quest.

On the way, the Argonauts rescued a blind prophet called Phineus from the Harpies, wicked monsters who snatched people. In return, Phineus told Jason to release a dove into the sky as the ship approached the fearsome Clashing Rocks that guarded the entrance to Colchis.

Jason did and the rocks parted to let the *Argo* through. Jason went to claim the golden fleece.

"I will give you the golden fleece," said King Aietes, "if you harness two fire-breathing bulls to plough a field. Then sow the field with dragons' teeth – each of which will grow into a fierce warrior."

With the help of Medea, Aietes' daughter who had fallen in love with him, Jason completed the task. Still Aietes wouldn't give up the fleece. Then Medea suggested he play music to lull the deadly serpent to sleep. It worked. At long last, Jason retrieved his prize!

Jason, Medea and the Argonauts set sail for Iolkos, and after many more adventures, they arrived safely. Brave, determined Jason finally claimed his throne and ruled for many years.

Make a Model Hurricane

A hurricane is the biggest and strongest of all storms, with powerful winds and torrential rain. It begins as a region of heated air over the warm waters of the tropics. The heated air expands and rises, creating an area of low pressure. As the surrounding air moves in towards the lower pressure, the Earth's rotation causes it to spin in a vortex. You can make a similar vortex in water.

You will need:
large bowl, water,
spoon, food colouring

1 Fill the bowl with lukewarm water. Use the spoon to stir the water so it moves in a circle around the bowl, creating a vortex.

2 Release a few drops of food colouring into the centre of the bowl. Watch the colour move out and form bands – just like the clouds in a hurricane.

Hurricane facts

■ The size of a hurricane can be up to 400 miles (650 km) in diameter.

■ As more and more air is drawn into the storm, the wind speeds increase.

■ Conditions in the eye (centre) of the storm are calm, while all around it are thick clouds and high-speed winds.

■ Wind speeds of 74 mph (118 kph) or over are classified as hurricane-force. Wind speeds have been known to reach up to 210 mph (350 km/h).

■ Hurricanes become stronger as they move over warm water, but gradually fade out over cool water or land.

Seasickness

Don't let it ruin your cruise!

Symptoms

* Nausea
* Headaches
* Stomach cramps
* Dizziness
* Vomiting

Cause

Seasickness is a form of motion sickness caused by the mismatch of information between your eyes and the balance system located in your inner ear. Your eyes detect that you are stationary, while your balance system senses motion.

Seasickness
Don't let it ruin your cruise!

How to avoid feeling seasick

✔ Keep busy and try to forget about it.

✔ Go out on the deck so you can adapt to being aboard the ship.

✔ Look at the horizon as a point of reference.

✔ Stay in an outside room with a window so you can see the horizon.

✔ The middle of the ship is more stable than the bow (front) or the stern (back).

✔ Try a seasickness remedy, suck boiled sweets or wear a seasickness wristband.

✔ Foods such as ginger, green apples and crackers may help reduce nausea.

> **!** CARRY A SICK BAG WITH YOU
> **■** IN CASE ALL ELSE FAILS!

Chapter 4

CRASH!

As the ship rolled violently, the crowd staggered this way and that through the lobby of Deck 11. Marina, Jason and Pearl were in the middle of it, cushioned by people on all sides.

"I hope Dad's okay," said Jason.

Marina nodded. She hoped so, too.

Suddenly the ship crashed into something.

THUD!

The force of the collision flung the crowd forwards and then back again.

"What was that?" asked Marina.

"The ship hit something." Jason's eyes were wide with fear. "It's just like the *Titanic*! We're going to sink!" His heart was pounding and for a moment, he felt as if he couldn't breathe.

Pearl squeezed his hand. "Don't panic. Be brave," she told him. "Remember, you're Jason, the seafaring hero."

He sighed deeply. He might not really be a hero, but if ever there was a time to be brave, this was it!

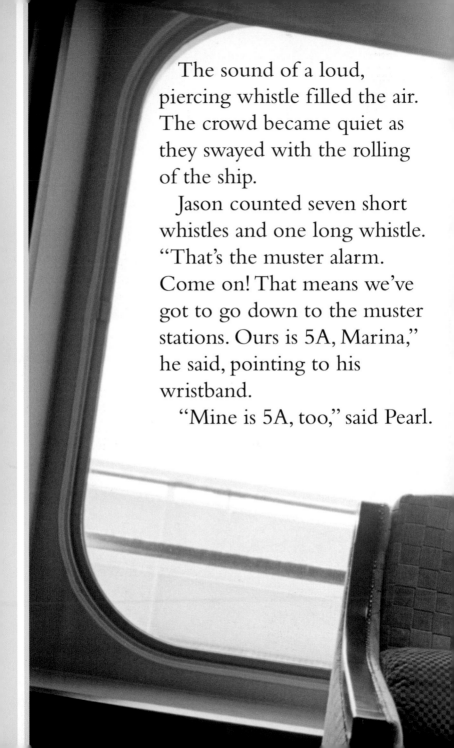

The sound of a loud, piercing whistle filled the air. The crowd became quiet as they swayed with the rolling of the ship.

Jason counted seven short whistles and one long whistle. "That's the muster alarm. Come on! That means we've got to go down to the muster stations. Ours is 5A, Marina," he said, pointing to his wristband.

"Mine is 5A, too," said Pearl.

"How do we get there? Do we need life jackets?" Marina asked. "What about—"

She was interrupted by Captain MacGill on the public address system. "Attention, please. We are abandoning ship. Please follow the crew's instructions and go to the muster stations on Deck 4 as quickly as possible, where lifeboats will be ready. Wear your life jacket if you have it with you. More life jackets are available at the muster stations."

The crowd started to panic. Some people started to run and push their way through, while others frantically called for family and friends.

Calmly, the ship's crew directed the frightened passengers towards their muster stations. The crowd separated into groups, following crew members holding up signs. The children and Pearl followed a crew member with a sign for Muster Station 5A. His badge said:

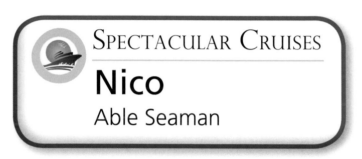

SPECTACULAR CRUISES

Nico

Able Seaman

Nico led the group down a stairwell. Tiny lights in the floor lit their way.

"It's a long walk down to the muster stations," said Nico, "but the lifts are out of operation for safety reasons."

The ship was still tossing and turning and they had to hold tightly to the railing so they didn't topple down the stairs.

"What about Dad?" asked Marina, as she followed Jason and Pearl. "How will he get to the muster station? You know how sick he was feeling."

"The ship's staff will check the cabins to make sure all of the passengers have got out," Pearl assured her.

"Maybe Dad's at the muster station already," said Jason hopefully.

At last they reached muster station 5A.

"Dad! Dad!" called Jason and Marina, scouring the crowd.

Pearl looked, too.

MUSTER STATION

Nico handed them each a big orange life jacket. "I'm sure you'll find your dad," he said, "but right now you've got to put these on and get in the lifeboat."

Jason pulled the life jacket over his head and buckled it around his chest and waist as they'd been shown at the muster drill. He checked that his life jacket had a light and a whistle attached.

With life jackets firmly fastened, Jason, Marina and Pearl lined up with the other passengers to get in a lifeboat.

Through the glass door that led outside, they could see sheets of rain and the wild, stormy sea crashing onto the deck.

"Stay calm, everyone. Wait your turn," the crew called to people pushing to the front of the line. "There are plenty of lifeboats and space for 150 people in each one."

"Dad!" called Jason to a man waiting ahead of them. But when the man turned around, it wasn't Dad after all.

"Maybe he's in one of those," said Pearl, pointing to the lifeboats being lowered into the water.

The lifeboats had waterproof coverings, so they couldn't see inside.

Quickly, the crew helped the passengers on board. Soon it was the turn of the children and Pearl.

As they stepped onto the outer deck of the ship, a gust of wind and rain hit them full in the face.

WHOOSH!

Marina held on tightly to Jason so he didn't blow over. They struggled into the lifeboat and strapped themselves in. Within ten minutes, the lifeboat was full, but there was still no sign of Dad.

Nico sat next to them.

"Why are we abandoning ship?" Jason asked him.

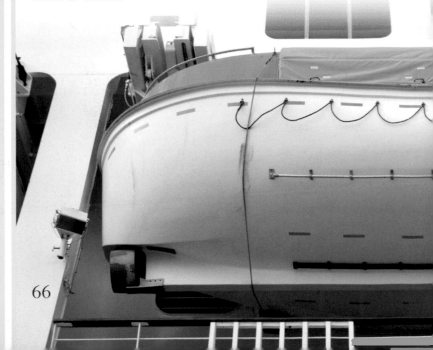

"The force of the wind and the waves pushed the ship into a submerged island," Nico replied. "The hull sustained damage in the crash and it's taking in water."

"Will the ship sink?" asked Jason.

"I don't know," said Nico. "The captain's not taking any chances."

Just then, the crew at the muster station zipped the door of the lifeboat shut like the door of a tent and the boat swayed in the wind as it was lowered towards the sea.

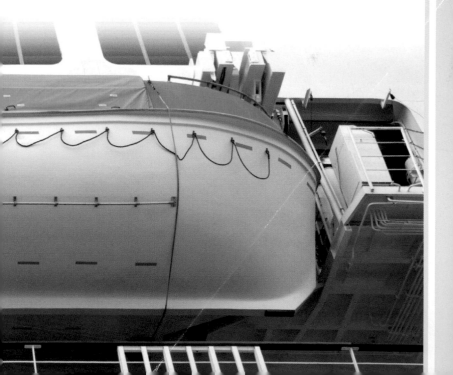

Emergency Information

Muster Drills

▲ All passengers are required by law to attend a muster drill. This is generally held prior to the ship's departure from port.

▲ Drills take place at or near muster stations, which are located next to lifeboat embarkation points where passengers have easy access.

▲ At the muster drill, passengers receive instructions on what to do in an emergency. However, they do not get in lifeboats during the muster drill.

Life jackets

▲ Cabins are equipped with life jackets for each passenger. More life jackets are stored at muster stations. You will learn how to put on your life jacket at the muster drill.

Lifeboats

▲ The ship's lifeboats have space for every person on board, plus additional capacity.

▲ In the unlikely event that we must abandon ship, it is vital to board lifeboats in a quick and orderly manner. Follow the crew's instructions!

On board the *Spectacular*

Crew

▲ Crew members are highly trained in emergency procedures, including evacuations and crowd control.

▲ Crew members regularly have lifeboat drills to practise launching and manouevring lifeboats.

▲ During an emergency, every member of the crew has specific duties so they all know exactly what to do.

The decision to evacuate is made by the captain who:

1 assesses the amount of damage the ship is able to withstand;

2 judges whether the ship is able to sail safely to the nearest port;

3 ensures that the safety of everyone on board is top priority.

Titanic

Intended voyage: Southampton, England across the north Atlantic to New York City, USA (April 1912)

Weather: clear and calm, but cold

Ship: 269 m (882 ft) long. The hull was divided into 15 bulkheads (vertical partitions) so that if one or two bulkheads flooded, the ship would still float – leading to the claim that the ship was 'virtually unsinkable'.

Passengers: 1,324 passengers (plus 898 crew). Many were emigrating to the United States. Divisions between 1st, 2nd and 3rd class passengers meant that lower class passengers couldn't make their way to the lifeboat deck.

Collision: scraped against an iceberg, making a number of long gashes in the hull, and flooding five of the bulkheads

Emergency procedures: neither crew nor passengers knew where to go or what to do.

Lifeboats: Only 20 lifeboats (not nearly enough). The crew lowered lifeboats into the water partly occupied.

Rescue: After several hours in the lifeboats in the cold ocean without food or fresh water, surviving passengers were finally rescued by the *Carpathia*, a nearby ship.

Intended voyage: Miami, Florida around the Bahama Islands in the Caribbean Sea and back to Miami

Weather: hurricane

Ship: 290 m (950 ft) long and 37 m (120 ft) wide, with 15 decks. The *Spectacular* would be an average size for a modern cruise ship. Since the *Titanic* disaster, international Safety of Life at Sea (SOLAS) regulations require ships to be equipped with numerous safety features.

Passengers: 3,000 (plus 1,050 crew). The passengers are all on a luxury holiday cruise.

Collision: crashed into a submerged island

Emergency procedures: SOLAS regulations require crews to undergo frequent in-depth training and to be assigned specific duties in emergencies. Passengers must attend a safety drill called a 'muster drill' to acquaint them with emergency procedures for unlikely occurrences such as shipwrecks, adverse weather, on-board fires, etc.

Lifeboats: 30 lifeboats to fit a total of 4,500 people (more than enough space for all of the passengers and crew).

Rescue: To be decided...

Chapter 5

INTO THE HURRICANE

The lifeboat reached the surface of the water and immediately started tossing and turning in the stormy sea. Marina clutched the armrests of her seat and thought about how calm and peaceful the ocean had been only yesterday. Now all she could see through the porthole was the driving rain and churning sea. Wave after giant wave carried the lifeboat up and over, rocking it and spinning it around. It was like the worst amusement park ride in the world. She hoped Dad would be okay.

The wind and waves battered the lifeboat nonstop. Inside, the passengers sat quietly reassuring each other. Marina guessed that many of them were trying not to be seasick. On one side of her, Pearl sat calmly. On the other side, Jason was watching Nico and Kelly, the two able seamen in charge of the lifeboat.

Nico took a long, red baton out of a storage locker and handed it to Kelly.

"What do you think that is?" Marina whispered to Jason.

"Maybe a flare?" he said.

Kelly unzipped a hatch in the waterproof covering and poked her head through. A moment later, the children saw bright red smoke shoot up into the sky, but it soon disappeared amid the dark clouds and heavy rain.

"Let's save the other emergency flares until the weather clears a bit," Kelly told Nico. "We don't want to waste them."

Next, they started the lifeboat's motor with the aim of sailing out of the hurricane, but it was no use against the force of the storm. They turned the motor off again to save the fuel for later.

"We'll have to wait out the storm," said Kelly.

Just then, the lifeboat plunged up and over another wave. Marina held her breath, afraid they might tip upside down, but luckily, the lifeboat righted itself.

She sighed impatiently. "We could be drifting around in this hurricane forever."

"It will pass eventually," Nico assured her. "Anyway, the lifeboat's fitted with automatic EPIRB."

"What's that?" asked Jason.

"Emergency Positioning Indicating Radio Beacon," Kelly answered. "It sends a distress message to the nearest rescue centre and also has built-in GPS so they can locate us."

"GPS stands for Global Positioning System," Jason told Marina, "like the satellite navigation in the car."

"I know what it is," she snapped.

Marina was quiet then. She just wanted to be back in the sunshine, on the big luxurious ship having a fantastic holiday with Dad. She didn't want to be rolling and spinning around in the lifeboat in the middle of a hurricane.

?
What does EPIRB stand for and what does it do?

Marina didn't know how much time had passed when Jason suddenly pointed out the porthole. "Look, there's the *Spectacular*! See how it's tilting."

She peered through the rain. Sure enough, the ship was tilting forwards and the front end was already under water. Marina could even make out the brightly coloured slides of the water park on the top deck, now partly submerged beneath the ocean. With each crash of the waves, the *Spectacular* tilted a little bit more.

Suddenly, Marina saw a bright red light shoot briefly into the sky. "Look, there's a flare! It must be from another lifeboat."

Jason, Nico and Kelly all looked through the porthole, as another flare flickered in the stormy sky.

Quickly, Kelly grabbed a whistle from the storage locker. She unzipped the hatch again and poked her head outside to blow the whistle. A moment later, another faint whistle sounded in reply, and then a second. All the passengers on the lifeboat cheered. It was comforting to know that they weren't alone in the vast, wild sea.

Nico handed Kelly a searchlight. The children watched through the porthole as the strong beam shone through the rain and clouds until it finally found two lifeboats.

"Maybe Dad's on one of those!" Marina said to Jason.

His face brightened. "Let's link our lifeboat with the others, Nico," he suggested. "That's what the people on the lifeboats from the *Titanic* did, and they're the ones who survived."

"The sea was calm the night the *Titanic* sank," said Nico. "They weren't sailing through a hurricane like this."

"It's worth a try, isn't it?" Marina urged.

"The children's dad might be on one of those lifeboats," Pearl pointed out.

Kelly came back inside. "The weather's dreadful out there, but I've managed to attach a flashing distress signal to the hook on top of our lifeboat so the other

78

lifeboats can see us. Their crews are doing the same."

"Good," said Nico. "We're going to try young Jason's idea and link up with them. We'll use a buoyant rope."

"A chain of lifeboats. Good idea," said Kelly. She retrieved a rope from the locker. White floats were attached at intervals and there were hooks at each end.

Nico grabbed the megaphone from the locker. "I'll suggest the plan to the crew in the other lifeboats. I hope they'll hear me over the noise of the storm."

Nico unzipped the hatch and poked his head out into the storm, clutching the megaphone. Through the howling wind and crashing waves, Marina and Jason could hear him call out the plan. They only hoped that the crews on the other lifeboats could hear it, too.

Nico came back inside. He handed Kelly the megaphone and she gave him the rope. Marina and Jason watched through the porthole as he hooked one end of the rope to a lifeline on the side of their lifeboat. Then he threw the other end towards one of the other lifeboats.

The wild waves carried the rope every which way, and Nico kept having to pull it in and throw it back out again.

At last the rope reached its target and the two lifeboats were linked.

?

What were the challenges of linking up lifeboats?

Again, the passengers cheered.

"What's your dad's name?" Nico asked Marina and Jason, as he leaned in to grab the megaphone.

"John Waverly," they replied together.

Nico called to the other crew through the megaphone. "Is there a man named John Waverly on your lifeboat?"

The children held their breaths.

"No, but he's on that other one nearby," came the answer.

Jason and Marina looked out the porthole. Through the rain, they spotted another flashing signal in the distance.

"There's Dad's lifeboat!" Jason exclaimed. "Let's link up with it!"

Nico unwound another buoyant rope, ready to throw it. Suddenly a huge wave crashed over the lifeboat, surging through

the hatch and drenching the passengers. Quickly, Nico dropped back inside the lifeboat and zipped the hatch back up. He was dripping too.

The children looked back through the porthole. They spotted one lifeboat heaving and pitching alongside them, linked by the buoyant rope, but the flashing signal of their dad's lifeboat was nowhere to be seen.

Lifeboat equipment checklist

Modern lifeboats must carry a range of emergency equipment as specified by SOLAS. About 40–50 different items are required, depending on the type of lifeboat. Here are some of the items.

- ☑ Lifebuoy
- ☑ Whistle
- ☑ Searchlight
- ☑ Food rations and water
- ☑ Compass
- ☑ Fire extinguisher
- ☑ First aid kit
- ☑ Fishing kit
- ☑ Jackknife
- ☑ Oars
- ☑ Sea anchor

Lifebuoy

Whistle

Searchlight

Food rations and water

Marine distress signals

Send an emergency signal to nearby boats and ships with a flare.

* Hand flare
* Rocket parachute flare
* Buoyant smoke signal

Hand flare

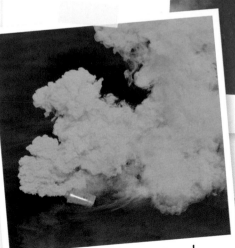

Buoyant smoke signal

Terrible Tropical Storms

Severe tropical storms are called hurricanes in the North Atlantic and Caribbean Sea, typhoons in the North Pacific, and cyclones in the South Pacific and Indian Ocean. Much of the damage is caused by dramatic high tides called storm surges.

NAME **Typhoon Wipha**

LOCATION **Northwest Pacific**

DATE **2013**

WIND SPEED **131 mph (212 km/h)**

Record rainfall in Japan due to Typhoon Wipha caused deadly mudslides. As the typhoon moved northwards, cold air turned the rain into a blinding snowstorm.

NAME **Cyclone Mahasen**

LOCATION **Bay of Bengal**

DATE **2013**

WIND SPEED **57 mph (93 km/h)**

Despite fading to a tropical storm by the time it hit landfall, Cyclone Mahasen still led to devastating floods and landslides in parts of Asia.

NAME **Hurricane Katrina**

LOCATION New Orleans, USA

DATE 2005

WIND SPEED 140 mph (225 km/h)

Storm surges broke through the city's flood defences, causing massive flooding that cost $108 billion (£69 billion) worth of damage. The city's flood defences have since been improved.

NAME **Hurricane Ike**

LOCATION Caribbean Sea

DATE 2008

WIND SPEED 143 mph (230 km/h)

In 2008, 16 tropical storms, including 8 full-scale hurricanes such as Ike, ripped through the Caribbean Sea, causing damage on many of the islands.

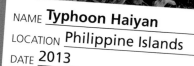

NAME **Typhoon Haiyan**

LOCATION Philippine Islands

DATE 2013

WIND SPEED 235 mph (380 km/h)

Between 20–25 tropical storms hit the Philippines every year, but Typhoon Haiyan was one of the worst, affecting 14 million people.

Wild Waves

The wind creates waves as it blows across the ocean's surface. As the wind gains strength, the ocean's surface gradually changes from flat and smooth to growing levels of roughness. Strong, persistent winds blowing over long distances form the biggest waves.

Wave Generation

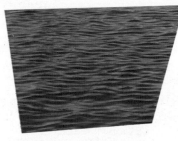

◄ A light wind creates ripples.

A stronger wind causes choppy water. ▶

◄ Wind speeds over 40 mph (60 km/h) can create very rough seas with waves several metres high.

▲ Chaotic waves

The area over which the wind blows is called the fetch. The ocean surface in the fetch is usually quite chaotic, with groups of waves of different sizes and wavelengths clashing and crashing. The stronger the wind, the more chaotic the waves become.

Chapter 6

Land Ahoy!

Marina and Jason gazed out of the porthole, searching for the flashing distress signal from their dad's lifeboat. Pearl looked, too, her calm presence giving them hope. Kelly unzipped the hatch to peer outside. Meanwhile, Nico passed around towels and blankets to keep everyone dry and warm. Water from the wave sloshed on the floor of the lifeboat.

"I'm sorry, kids, but I don't see your dad's lifeboat," said Kelly at last, coming back inside. "I'm sure we'll see it when the hurricane passes."

"When will that be?" snapped Jason.

Pearl patted his hand. "We all hope the hurricane will pass soon, but we can't control the weather."

"What we can do is stay strong," said Nico. "You must all be hungry."

He passed around energy bars and bottles of water from the storage locker. The children hadn't realised how hungry they were, and now they ate quickly while still keeping a watch through the porthole.

Outside the lifeboat, the stormy sky was growing even darker as night set in. Jason felt sleepy. He curled up between Marina and Pearl and closed his eyes. Marina was tired too, but she tried to stay awake so she could keep searching for Dad's lifeboat.

"Don't worry, dear," Pearl whispered to her. "I'll keep looking for you."

"Thanks." Marina sighed, and soon she was asleep, too.

Jason woke up first. He looked around and wondered where he was.

"You're on the lifeboat," Pearl told him, as if reading his mind.

Around them, most of the other passengers were asleep.

"Where's Dad?" said Marina, rubbing her eyes and stretching.

"I'm afraid we haven't spotted any other lifeboats. Just the one that's linked up with us," said Pearl. "But I'm sure we will soon. Look through the porthole."

Jason and Marina looked outside. They couldn't believe their eyes. The thick grey clouds, driving rain and rough seas had disappeared. The sky was bright blue with only a few wispy clouds in sight, and the

calm, tranquil ocean
seemed to sparkle in
the sunshine. It was
as if the hurricane
had never happened.

"Marina, feel the
lifeboat!" Jason
exclaimed. "It's not
going crazy in the wind
and waves anymore."

Marina smiled. "You're right. We're just
bobbing along gently now."

"I hope this means Dad's not feeling
seasick anymore," he added.

"I'm sure he's better now," said Marina.

The children were both quiet for a
moment as they gazed out at the shining
blue sea. On the water's surface, they
could see the white floats of the buoyant
rope linking them to the other lifeboat
that bobbed alongside them. But where
was Dad's lifeboat?

"Morning, kids," said Kelly, as she poked her head through the hatch. A pair of binoculars hung around her neck.

"We told you the hurricane would pass eventually." Nico winked at the children and passed Kelly a flare.

A moment later, a bright red light shot up into the clear blue sky. Another flare, with orange smoke curling up into the sky, went up from the other lifeboat.

"Someone's bound to see us now," said Pearl. "We'll be rescued soon!"

"Look!" called Jason, pointing through the porthole. "The dolphins are here!"

Sure enough, a pod of 50 or more dolphins was swimming into view.

Marina was so glad to see them. She watched as the dolphins swam in formation, leaping and diving, one after the other in a line.

"It's almost as if they want us to follow them," she said.

Jason jumped up. "You're right, Marina! I read stories in my dolphin book about how they can help humans in trouble."

He ran over to Nico and Kelly. "We've got to follow the dolphins. They'll take us to safety. I know they will!"

"Have the dolphins come to rescue us then?" said Nico with a grin.

"Jason's right," said Kelly. "Look through the binoculars, Nico. There's land ahoy, and the dolphins are leading us straight to it!"

Quickly, Nico started the lifeboat motor, while Kelly used the megaphone to tell the crew in the other lifeboat what was happening. Soon, both lifeboats were speeding along after the dolphins, heading for land.

"Who knows?" Pearl said to the children. Her eyes sparkled like the sea. "Perhaps we're about to find Atlantis!"

"What's that?" asked Jason.

"It's supposed to be a lost island," said Pearl. "Some people think it might be somewhere in the Caribbean Sea."

As they got nearer, the children could see a sandy beach fringed by tall palm trees. At last the crews anchored the lifeboats and everyone waded through the clear, shallow water onto the beach.

Marina and Jason watched the dolphins swim away.

"Thank you!" Jason called after them. "Can you go and find our dad now, please? Make sure he's okay."

The ancient Greek philosopher, Plato, told this story about 2,400 years ago. Is it true? Or is it a fable that teaches a lesson? **What do you think?**

ATLANTIS

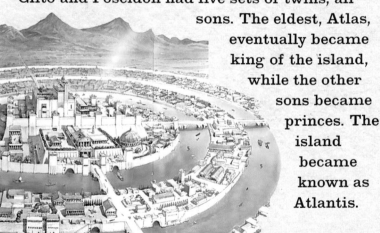

POSEIDON, the great god of the sea, fell in love with Clito, a human woman, and built her a house on a high hill in the middle of an island. He made the island into a lush paradise, with fertile fields and tall forests, and surrounded it with rings of water and land. Clito and Poseidon had five sets of twins, all sons. The eldest, Atlas, eventually became king of the island, while the other sons became princes. The island became known as Atlantis.

98

The people of Atlantis lived in peace and prosperity. However, as generations passed, succeeding kings wanted to add to the wealth of the kingdom. The original home at the centre of the island became a palace covered in gold. Bridges were built connecting the rings of water and land to create a large city. A great harbour allowed riches to be imported to Atlantis from faraway places. The more the people of Atlantis had, the more they wanted. Once they had lived together in harmony, but now greed and envy took over.

Poseidon decided to put a stop to it. The great god of the sea created a gigantic wave, even taller than the forest and higher than the high hill in the middle of the island. The gigantic wave crashed over the island, burying Atlantis beneath the ocean forever more.

Is Atlantis real? If so, where is it? Some people think it's beneath the Atlantic Ocean near the island of Bimini in the Bermuda Triangle. In 1968, an underwater causeway and building were discovered there. Although experts found that the Bimini Road causeway is a natural rock formation and the underwater building is from the 1930s, believers still think that energy crystals from Atlantis interfere with ships and aircraft in the Bermuda Triangle.

Saved by Dolphins

Read these experiences of people who have been saved by dolphins. These are all true stories, EXCEPT for one. Which experience is false?

See page 125 for the answer.

DOLPHIN RESCUES BOY

In 2000, Davide Ceci fell out of his father's fishing boat off the coast of Italy. Davide didn't know how to swim, but was saved when a dolphin pushed him up out of the water towards the boat so his father could pull him back in to safety.

DOLPHINS SHOW THE WAY

In 2004, 12 scuba divers were swept away from their boat in the Red Sea. Rescuers searched but couldn't find them – until a group of dolphins jumped over the prow of the rescue boat, all in the same direction. They followed the dolphins and found the scuba divers.

DOLPHINS KEEP DIVER AFLOAT

In 2006, Matthew Harvey was knocked unconscious while scuba diving. After about 56 hours in the water, the crew of a passing yacht spotted him, surrounded by dolphins who were apparently keeping him afloat.

DOLPHINS SAVE SURFER

Todd Endris was surfing off the coast of California in 2007 when a shark attacked him. Then a pod of dolphins swam up and surrounded him, protecting him from the shark until he was able to surf back to the safety of the beach.

DOLPHIN HERO

In 2008, an eyewitness in the Philippine Islands saw a large dolphin push fisherman Joseph Cesdorio on to the shore in an attempted rescue after his fishing boat capsized in a typhoon. Sadly, neither Cesdorio nor the dolphin survived the ordeal.

DOLPHIN RIDE

In 2015, Juan Rivera and his sister, Felicia, had drifted far away from the beach in Mexico. Suddenly, two dolphins nudged the children with their beaks. Juan and Felicia climbed on to the dolphins' backs, and the dolphins gave them a ride safely back to the beach.

101

Chapter 7

RESCUE

Between the two lifeboats, there were 300 people on the beach. Jason and Marina were so relieved to be on land, they took their shoes off and ran barefoot across the white sand. Pearl laughed.

"What a gorgeous island," said Marina. "I just wish Dad was here with us."

?

How did Jason and Marina feel when they arrived on the island? How would you feel?

"Put your shoes back on and let's go exploring," Pearl suggested.

They told Nico and Kelly what they were going to do.

"Don't go too far," Kelly told them. "Come back to the beach when you see an orange smoke flare."

They headed towards the lush, green interior of the island. Above them, birds chirped and flitted about.

"Are you okay, Pearl?" asked Marina, after a while.

Scrambling through the thick foliage was hard work.

"I'm fine, dear," Pearl replied. "When I was a child, I longed to have an adventure on a deserted island."

"Like Robinson Crusoe!" said Jason. "I love that book."

"Me too," Pearl agreed. "In fact, the story is based on a sailor called Alexander Selkirk who really did live on a deserted island."

"Really? Cool!" Jason ducked under the low-hanging branch of a tree. "I'm hungry. What do you think Alexander Selkirk ate on his island?"

Just then, they came through the thicket to a field of tall, wild grass.

"Look, it's perfect," laughed Pearl. "Let's have a snack."

"A snack of what?" asked Marina.

Pearl pulled up a stalk of the tall grass. "This is sugar cane. If you chew on it, you'll get some of the sugary sweetness that's inside. Just don't eat this tough stem." She showed them how to do it.

"Mmm, that's good," said Jason.

"Better than the energy bar we had last night," Marina agreed.

Suddenly they spotted an orange smoking flare shooting into the sky.

"We'd better get back to the beach," said Marina.

"Maybe Dad's lifeboat is there!" Jason started running back the way they had come. The others followed.

There were now at least a dozen lifeboats anchored off the beach and crowds of people from the *Spectacular* milling about on the sand.

"Dad! Dad!" the children yelled.

"John Waverly," called Pearl. "Are you here? John Waverly?"

They were full of hope as they wandered around the crowd, searching for their dad and calling his name.

Marina spotted Nico and Kelly with sheets of paper on a clipboard. "Have you seen our dad? Is he here?"

"Not yet," said Nico. "We're making a list of everyone arriving on the island in a lifeboat, and we've been keeping a special eye out for your dad."

"We'll let you know as soon as we see him," added Kelly. "Captain MacGill isn't here yet either."

"How did these lifeboats manage to find the island?" Pearl asked them.

"The dolphins, of course!" said Jason.

Nico smiled. "Some lifeboat crews tracked us here on GPS and others saw our flares."

"One way or another, I hope—" Marina began.

All of a sudden, Jason spotted the dolphins, and behind them, another lifeboat. "There he is! Dad! Dad!"

Jason dashed across the beach into the shallow water, with Marina splashing along close behind.

"Kids! Wait for the boat to anchor, then we'll see if your dad's on it," Kelly called after them.

Pearl watched with a smile as the children raced towards the lifeboat.

"They'll be fine now," she said.

"Marina! Jason!" called their dad from the lifeboat. He jumped in the water and swam towards the children.

"Are you still seasick, Dad?" asked Jason, giving him a wet cuddle.

Marina laughed. She was certainly glad to see him.

Dad laughed too. "No, I'm not seasick now," he said, "but you should have seen me on the lifeboat!"

Throughout the afternoon, the rest of the lifeboats arrived from the *Spectacular,* including Captain MacGill's.

"Don't we need to make shelters if we're going to stay on the island?" Jason asked the captain.

"Or should we all get in the lifeboats and sail back to Grand Bahama Island?" Marina asked her.

They were sitting on the beach with their dad and Pearl, chewing on some sugar cane.

"We won't need to do that," Captain MacGill replied.

Just then, they heard a whirring sound and a helicopter hovered into view over the island.

"Look there!" Pearl exclaimed, pointing towards the sea.

?

What do you think Pearl has spotted in the sea?

A fleet of rescue boats could be seen on the horizon. The beach erupted in cheers from the *Spectacular's* 3,000 passengers and 1,050 crew, as the rescue boats sped across the sea towards the island.

Soon Marina and Jason were on the deck of a rescue boat with their dad. They didn't want to let him out of their sight.

"That was certainly an exciting cruise, wasn't it?" said Dad.

"We'll have to write Mum another postcard," laughed Marina. "We have so much to tell her!"

Jason gazed out at the enormous ocean that spread out all around them. "I wonder where the *Spectacular* is?"

"At the bottom of the sea, I guess," said Dad.

"But where exactly?" Jason persisted. "How could such a huge ship disappear?"

"Maybe some day we'll find it, Jason," Marina said to her brother.

Jason nodded. "Yes, some day."

Alexander Selkirk:
The Real Robinson Crusoe

In 1719, author Daniel Defoe wrote the classic adventure novel, *Robinson Crusoe*, about a man stranded on a deserted island. Experts believe that Defoe based his story on the adventures of Scottish sailor Alexander Selkirk…

AYE, so you want to know a wee bit about how I came to be stranded on my island. I was a good sailor, and a good navigator, though a bit hotheaded. In 1704, I was on the crew of a ship called the *Cinque Ports*. Captain Stradling was young and arrogant, only 21 years old. Most of the crew had more sailing experience than he! We had been hired by the British crown to raid Spanish ships and villages around the coast of South America.

When we discovered that worms were eating through the wooden ship, we docked on a deserted island for repairs. The ship was in a bad state and I told Captain Stradling that it wasn't seaworthy. Most of the crew seemed to agree, but Captain Stradling stood firm. We argued and I told Stradling that I'd rather stay on the deserted island than sail a leaky ship. I thought the crew would agree with me, but they all followed the captain back on board the ship. Stradling took great pleasure in leaving me stranded!

I expected to be found within a few days. In fact, it was five long years. I built a shelter near a stream, ate fish and wild goat, and foraged for fruit and vegetables. Oh, how I craved foods like bread and salt! I kept a close watch for ships on the horizon, though I hid if I saw a Spanish one. In time, I got used to life on my island, but it was still a joy when Captain Woodes Rogers rescued me in his ship the *Duke*!

I learned that the *Cinque Ports* had indeed sunk and only Captain Stradling and a few others had survived. So my sailor's instincts had saved me! When I returned to Britain, I became famous. I was interviewed for *The Englishman* magazine and became the inspiration for the best-selling novel, *Robinson Crusoe*.

AYE, BUT MINE IS THE TRUE TALE!

Search and Rescue

Luckily, the lifeboats from the *Spectacular* were all fitted with EPIRB so rescue services in the United States could easily find them.

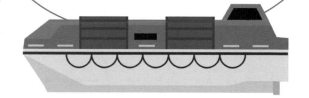

1 The EPIRB transmitted a distress signal from the lifeboats to a satellite, probably one belonging to NOAA, which usually transmits weather information.

- **EPIRB** – Emergency Position Indicating Radio Beacon

- **NOAA** – National Oceanic and Atmospheric Association Monitors changes to the environment, including weather and conditions at sea.

- **SARSAT** – Search and Rescue Satellite Aided Tracking Part of NOAA, the SARSAT system locates people in distress on land, at sea and in the air.

2 The satellite pinpointed the location to within 50 m (164 ft) using GPS. Each EPIRB is licenced to a specific boat, so the satellite could also identify it.

3 The location was relayed to the SARSAT Mission Control at NOAA's Satellite Operations Centre in Maryland, USA.

4 SARSAT Mission Control contacted the nearest United States Coast Guard Rescue Coordination Centre. In the case of the *Spectacular*, these were located in Miami, Florida and San Juan, Puerto Rico.

5 The Search and Rescue team was on its way!

Surviving at Sea Game

1	Having a fantastic cruise with Dad. Go forward 3 spaces.	**3**	Spot dolphins breaching. Go forward 2 spaces.	**5**
20 Thick fog means you skip a turn.	**19**	**18** Delicious breakfast buffet! Go forward 5 spaces.	**17**	**16**
21	**22** You've sailed into a hurricane! Go back 3 spaces.	**23**	**24** The ship crashes into a submerged island. Go back 8 spaces.	**25**
You're in the eye of the hurricane. Skip a turn.	**39**	The lifeboat is equipped with EPIRB and GPS. Go forward 7 spaces.	**37**	**36**
41	You've linked up with another lifeboat. Go forward 5 spaces.	**43**	Stay to look for Dad's lifeboat. Skip a turn.	**45**
Land ahoy! You've made it to the island. Well done!	**59** A water spout blocks your way. Go back 9 spaces.	**58**	**57**	**56**

116

Who will reach the island first?

To play, you will need: counters for each player; dice

6	7	8	9	
		You're sailing through the Bermuda Triangle! Go back 5 spaces.		Skip a turn while you investigate a possible UFO.
15	You're feeling seasick. Go back 7 spaces.	13	Choppy seas. Go back 3 spaces.	11
26	27	28 The captain gives the order to abandon ship. Skip a turn.	29	You paid attention at the muster drill and put on your life jacket. Go forward 5 spaces.
35	The weather is so bad that your flare can't be seen. Go back 8 spaces.	33	Everyone boards the lifeboat quickly and safely. Go forward 4 spaces.	31
46	47	48 The Gulf Stream carries you off course. Go back 2 spaces.	49	50
55	Pod of dolphins shows the way to the island. Go forward 2 spaces.	53	52	It's clear, sunny weather. Full speed ahead! Go forward 4 spaces.

Take turns rolling the dice. Follow the instructions in the squares. The player who reaches the island first wins the game.

117

Preparing for the Expedition

Jason and Marina had many years of education and training to prepare for their search for the sunken ship *Spectacular*.

Scuba diving

Marina and Jason took a scuba diving course at their local swimming pool. Once they learnt to use basic scuba equipment, they progressed to an open water dive course. They loved exploring under the sea and as they grew up, they went on many diving expeditions around the world.

More cruises

Over the years, Marina and Jason took many more cruises in different parts of the world. Sometimes they went with their dad (who eventually conquered his seasickness!) or their mum, and sometimes with Pearl. Jason even decided that the Bermuda Triangle was not unlucky after all.

Sea Scouts

Once they were old enough, Marina and Jason joined the Sea Scouts, where they learnt about ships and sailing. Both children advanced through the ranks to become Quartermaster Scouts.

University

• Marina attended the United States Coast Guard Academy. She became an expert sailor and served with the US Coast Guard for five years, participating in many rescues.
• Jason's love of reading helped him to earn high marks. He studied Marine Science at Florida Institute of Technology, where he learnt about the geography and environment of the oceans.

At last Marina and Jason decided they were ready to organise their expedition...

Jason's Expedition Journal

Marina and I are in the Bahamas with our expedition team. Tomorrow we set off to find the *Spectacular!* We've calculated where the ship would be if it was sailing at a speed of 22 knots when we encountered the hurricane. Of course, we don't know how far the hurricane pushed us off course...

Day 1

We set off early on our specially adapted fishing boat, the *Jasarina*. No sign of a shipwreck so far, although we've seen fascinating fish and coral on the underwater video camera. We've also seen some submerged islands.

I wonder which of these submerged islands the ship crashed into during the hurricane.

Day 2

Today, a pod of dolphins put on a show for us! The Caribbean Sea is full of islands fringed by palm trees, but which is the island that the dolphins led us to? As for the *Spectacular*, there's no trace yet. It was such a huge ship – where is it?

Day 3

Bingo! Marina spotted a tube that might be part of the water slide. We're about to put on our scuba gear so we can dive down and investigate.

Later...I think Marina was right! We found some sections of what must be the slide. The ocean floor plunges much deeper in that area, and we can see there's something down in the trench. We'll anchor here tonight and go down in the submersible tomorrow.

Day 4

We've found the *Spectacular*! We manoeuvred the submersible down into the trench and there it was! The ship was standing on its end, with the bow (front) buried in sand at the very bottom of the

trench and the stern (back) at the top. It's so strange seeing the cruise ship again, deep down under the ocean.

Day 5

We'll post photos of the *Spectacular* shipwreck on our blog and send the link to Captain MacGill. Marina and I might even organise another expedition to bring some objects back up to the surface. Or perhaps we should leave the ship alone now that we've found it? I can't decide...

Shipwreck Quiz

Can you find the answers to these questions about what you have read?

1. About how many islands are in the Bahamas?

2. What is a 'muster drill'?

3. What is a group of dolphins called?

4. If a dolphin 'breaches', what is it doing?

5. In which year did the *Titanic* set sail?

6. Where did the *Titanic's* voyage begin?

7. What are the three points of the Bermuda Triangle?

8. Which character feels seasick and misses breakfast?

9. According to Pearl, what does the name 'Marina' mean?

10. In the ancient Greek myth, what is the name of Jason's ship?

11. What is another name for the centre of a hurricane?

12. How many whistles is a muster alarm?

13. How many people fit in each of the *Spectacular's* lifeboats?

14. What is Nico's job on the *Spectacular*?

15. What does GPS stand for?

16. What is a severe tropical storm called in the South Pacific?

17. What creates waves in the ocean?

18. Alexander Selkirk's story is said to be the inspiration for which classic book of 1719?

19. What sweet treat did the children and Pearl have for a snack on the island?

20. What does SARSAT stand for?

Answers on page 125.

123

Glossary

Archipelago Group of islands.

Autopilot Controlled or driven by computers.

Buoyant Able to float.

Embark Start a journey.

Equator Imaginary line that divides Earth in half.

Flare Emergency device to attract attention with smoke or bright light.

Hull Main body of the ship.

Knot Speed in water, one nautical mile per hour.

Liner Large passenger ship.

Muster drill Safety drill.

Muster station Place for passengers to gather in an emergency.

Navigate Direct the route from one place to another.

Seaworthy Safe for a sea voyage.

Spectacular Extremely large, colourful or exciting.

Submerged Under the surface of the water.

Synchronised Actions having organised timing.

Trench Deep, steep-sided underwater valley.

Tropics Hot, usually sunny regions located near the Equator.

Submersible Vessel used to explore under the ocean.

Vortex Air or water whirling around the centre.

124

Index

Answer to pages 100–101: Dolphin Ride

Answers to the Shipwreck Quiz:
1. 700; **2.** Safety drill; **3.** Pod or school; **4.** Leaping into the air; **5.** 1912; **6.** Southampton, England; **7.** Bermuda, Puerto Rico and Miami, Florida; **8.** Dad; **9.** Lady of the sea; **10.** *Argo*; **11.** Eye of the hurricane; **12.** Seven short whistles and one long whistle; **13.** 150; **14.** Able seaman; **15.** Global Positioning System; **16.** Cyclone; **17.** Wind; **18.** *Robinson Crusoe*; **19.** Sugar cane; **20.** Search and Rescue Satellite Aided Tracking.

Guide for Parents

DK Reads is a three-level interactive reading adventure series for children, developing the habit of reading widely for both pleasure and information. These chapter books have an exciting main narrative interspersed with a range of reading genres to suit your child's reading ability, as required by the National Curriculum. Each book is designed to develop your child's reading skills, fluency, grammar awareness, and comprehension in order to build confidence and engagement when reading.

Ready for a *Reading Alone* book

YOUR CHILD SHOULD

- be able to read independently and silently for extended periods of time.
- read aloud flexibly and fluently, in expressive phrases with the listener in mind.
- respond to what they are reading with an enquiring mind.

A VALUABLE AND SHARED READING EXPERIENCE

Supporting children when they are reading proficiently can encourage them to value reading and to view reading as an interesting, purposeful and enjoyable pastime. So here are a few tips on how to use this book with your child.

TIP 1 Reading aloud as a learning opportunity:

- if your child has already read some of the book, ask him/her to explain the earlier part briefly.
- encourage your child to read slightly slower than his/her normal silent reading speed so that the words are clear and the listener has time to absorb the information, too.

Reading aloud provides your child with practice in expressive reading and performing to a listener, as well as a chance to share his/her responses to the storyline and the information.

TIP 2 Praise, share and chat:

- encourage your child to recall specific details after each chapter.
- provide opportunities for your child to pick out interesting words and discuss what they mean.
- discuss how the author captures the reader's interest, or how effective the non-fiction layouts are.
- ask the questions provided on some pages and in the quiz. These help to develop comprehension skills and awareness of the language used.
- ask if there's anything that your child would like to discover more about.

Further information can be researched in the index of other non-fiction books or on the Internet.

A FEW ADDITIONAL TIPS

- Continue to read to your child regularly to demonstrate fluency, phrasing and expression; to find out or check information; and for sharing enjoyment.
- Encourage your child to read a range of different genres, such as newspapers, poems, review articles and instructions.
- Provide opportunities for your child to read to a variety of eager listeners, such as a sibling or a grandparent.

Series consultant **Shirley Bickler** is a longtime advocate of carefully crafted, enthralling texts for young readers. Her LIFT initiative for infant teaching was the model for the National Literacy Strategy Literacy Hour, and she is co-author of *Book Bands for Guided Reading* published by Reading Recovery based at the Institute of Education.

Have you read these other great books from DK?

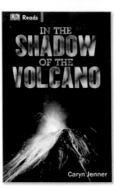

Dramatic modern-day adventure as Mount Vesuvius re-awakens.

Discover what life for pilots, women and children was like during WWII.

Pulse-racing action adventure chasing twisters in Tornado Alley.

Time-travelling adventure to the Wild West caught up in fossil hunters' rivalry.

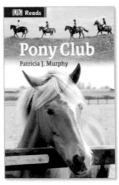

Emma adores horses. Will her wish come true at a riding camp?

Lucy follows her dream to train as a professional dancer.